★ 'The Chicken gave it to me'

Also by Anne Fine

'The Chicken gave it to me'

ANNE FINE

Illustrated by Philippe Dupasquier

EGMONT

For Clare Druce

You can visit Anne Fine's website
www.annefine.co.uk

and download free bookplates from
www.myhomelibrary.org

EGMONT
We bring stories to life

First published in Great Britain 1992
by Methuen Children's Books
This edition published 2010
by Egmont UK Limited
239 Kensington High Street
London W8 6SA

Text copyright © Anne Fine 1992
Illustrations copyright © Philippe Dupasquier 1992

The moral rights of the author and illustrator have been asserted

ISBN 978 1 4052 3321 7

3 5 7 9 10 8 6 4 2

A CIP catalogue record for this title is available from the British Library

Typeset by Avon DataSet Ltd, Bidford on Avon, Warwickshire
Printed and bound in Great Britain by the CPI Group

Contents

1
A tiny little book

Andrew laid it on Gemma's desk. A cloud of
farmyard dust puffed up in her face. The
first thing she asked when she stopped
sneezing was:

'Where did you get that?'

'The chicken gave it to me.'

'What chicken? How could a chicken
give it to you? It's a *book*.'

It was, too. A tiny little book. The cover
was just a bit of old farm sack with edges
that looked as if they had been – yes –
pecked. And the writing was all thin and

scratchy and – there's no way round this – *chickeny*.

'This is ridiculous! Chickens can't write books. Chickens can't *read*.'

'The chicken gave it to me,' Andrew repeated helplessly.

'But *how*?'

So Andrew told her how he'd been walking past the fence that ran round the farm sheds, and suddenly this chicken had leaped out in front of him in the narrow pathway.

'Pounced on me, really.'

'Don't be silly, Andrew. Chickens don't pounce.'

'This one did,' Andrew said stubbornly. 'It fluttered and squawked and made the most tremendous fuss. I was quite frightened. And it kept pushing this book at me with its scabby little foot – just pushing the book towards me whichever way I stepped. The chicken was absolutely determined I should take it.'

Gemma sat back in her desk and stared. She stared at Andrew as if she'd never even seen him before, as if they hadn't been sharing a desk for weeks and weeks, borrowing each other's rubbers, getting on one another's nerves, telling each other secrets. She thought she knew him well. Had he gone *mad*?

'Have you gone *mad*?'

Andrew leaned closer and hissed rather fiercely in her ear.

'Listen,' he said. 'I didn't *choose* to do this, you know. I didn't *want* this to happen. I didn't get out of bed this morning and fling back the curtains and say to myself, "Heigh-ho! What a great day to walk to school down the path by the farm sheds, minding my own business, and get attacked by some ferocious hen who has decided I

am the one to read his wonderful book –"'

'Her wonderful book,' interrupted Gemma. 'Hens aren't him. They're all her. That's how they get to lay eggs.'

Andrew chose to ignore this.

'Well,' he said. 'That's what happened. Believe me or don't believe me. I don't care. I'm simply telling you that this chicken stood there making a giant fuss and kicking up a storm until I reached down to pick up her dusty little book. Then she calmed down and strolled off.'

'Not strolled, Andrew,' Gemma said. 'Chickens don't stroll. She may have strutted off. Or even –'

But Andrew had shoved his round little face right up close to Gemma's, and he was hissing again.

'Gemma! This is *important*. Don't you *see*?'

And, all at once, Gemma believed him. Maybe she'd gone mad too. She didn't know. But she didn't think Andrew was making it up, and she didn't think Andrew was dreaming.

The chicken gave it to him.

She picked it up. More dust puffed out as, carefully, she stretched the sacking cover flat on her desk to read the scratchy chicken writing of the title.

The True Story Of Harrowing Farm

Opening it to the first page, she slid the book until it was exactly halfway between the two of them.

Together they began to read.

2
The True Story of Harrowing Farm

It was a wet and windy night, so wet you could slip and drown, so windy no one would hear your cries. Only a snake or a toad would choose to be away from shelter on such a night. And that is why only the snakes and the toads saw the gleaming green light pouring down from the black sky.

We chickens saw nothing, of course. How could we? There are no windows in the chicken shed. If we had windows, our lives could not be ruled so well by the electric light that decides when we wake and when we sleep and when we lay our eggs. After – oh, yes, of course, *after* – some of the hens in the cages by the door said that they'd heard the soft hum of the engines over the howling

of the wind. But the rest of us think they were boasting. On that black night, the spaceship landed without a sound. And it was not until the shed door flew open, flooding us with an eerie green light, that most of us chickens woke with a flutter and a squawk.

Little green men.

And they spoke perfect Chicken. (Later we found out they spoke Pig and Cow and Crow and pretty well everything. It's one of the ways in which they are, as they put it, 'superior'. They can speak any language they happen to meet. But on that first night we were amazed that they spoke perfect Chicken.)

Not that they were polite with it.

'Chickens!' said the spindliest and greenest, and it was almost like a groan. 'Travel a frillion miles, and what do you find when you arrive? A chicken!'

The others flicked the catches of our cage doors with their willowy green fingers.

'Out, out!' they called. 'Wakey, wakey! Make room! Out you get! Clear off! Go and make your own nests! The party's over!'

The party's over? We chickens couldn't believe our luck. We'd been locked in those cages almost since we were born. Nothing to do. You can't even stretch your wings. You just stand there on a wire rack (*ruining* your feet) for your whole life. And the one thing they want you to do – laying your egg – you'd far rather do in private.

The party's over! I can't describe to you the din as we all fluttered clumsily down,

and scrambled unsteadily for the door.

The little green men were even ruder now.

'Call themselves chickens? I've seen finer specimens on other planets begging to be put down!'

'Look at them! Twisted feet. Bare patches all over. And look at their beaks!'

'Disgusting!'

'Leave the door open as you go, please. This shed needs some fresh air.'

Fresh air! And we were out in it for the first time in our lives. We weren't going to hang around shutting the shed door. No fear. We were away. The last I heard as I went hobbling off on my poor feet into the night was one of the little green men scolding the stragglers.

'Hurry up. Out of those cages, *please*! We need them for others.'

With one last shudder and a flutter, I was off.

3

Harpoon . . . Harpsichord . . . Harridan . . .

Gemma read faster than Andrew. By the time he reached the bottom of the page, her eyes were already on him.

'What do you think?'

He twisted his face into a worried frown. He was about to speak, she knew. But then he just shook his head. He couldn't find the words.

'You think the chicken might have come from one of the farm sheds you pass on the way to school, don't you?' said Gemma. 'I didn't know the place had a name.'

Andrew turned back a page.

'Harrowing Farm . . .' he read aloud. 'Funny name.'

'Not *funny*,' said Gemma. 'That's just what harrowing *doesn't* mean.'

'Harrowing means raking,' Andrew corrected her. 'A harrow is a tool that breaks up lumps in the soil.'

Now it was Gemma's turn to correct him.

'When we went to London,' she told him, 'my dad wouldn't let me go in the Chamber of Horrors. He said it would be too harrowing.'

Andrew lifted his desk lid and rooted in the mess till he found his dictionary.

'Harpoon . . . harpsichord . . . harridan . . .' His finger slid down the side of the page. 'Here we are. Harrowing.'

She leaned across, but he lifted the book and turned to face her so she couldn't

see. She just had to listen to him reading it.

'*Harrowing: breaking the clods in soil; or: terribly upsetting and distressing.*'

Gemma ran her finger over the rough edge of the sacking cover.

'So which do you think they meant?'

'Maybe they meant both.'

'Oh, Andrew! Surely not! Farms aren't . . . Farms shouldn't be . . . Why, everyone knows that farms are . . .'

Even before her voice trailed away, she was out of her seat and over to the bookshelf. Her fingers ran across the spines of the books as she read the titles aloud:

'*Life in the Arctic . . . China . . . Pterodactyls . . . Meet the Stone Age People . . . On the Farm.* Here it is!'

She pulled out *On the Farm.* The book was for younger children really, but since the pictures were bright and clear, and there was quite a lot of information in it, their teacher had left it in the class library instead of sending it back to the Infants.

Gemma opened the pages at random. The pig was rooting contentedly with its snout in a frosty tussock of grass. The cow stood beside her calf, nudging her affectionately out of the ditch beside the hedge. In the soft summer evening sunlight, the hen ran happily round the orchard with her chicks.

'Well!' Andrew said. 'The farm doesn't look like that. It never has.'

Andrew should know. He'd walked past every day since he was five. There were no orchards, no hedges, no ditches, not even any tussocks of grass. There was fencing – miles of it to keep people out, and the land behind lay as flat and boring as a huge square of giant's knitting. When Andrew thought about it, he realised he only knew it was a farm at all because he had been told.

You never saw an animal as you passed by. All you saw standing in rows on the far side were six great long brown sheds.

'The sheds! They're not at all like the ones in this book.'

He pointed to the page with the picture of the pig. The shed behind stood crooked, with a drooping roof. Some of the tiles had slipped, leaving holes over the slats. The door hung on one hinge. And all around lay stones from a low wall outside that had tumbled down long ago.

And everywhere was green. Green, green, green, green. The shed was drowning in green – strangled with brambles, choked with weeds, surrounded by nettles, crowned with moss.

'You could muck about in that shed for hours. Days! Weeks! *Years!*'

'No wonder the pig looks happy . . .'

She sounded so wistful. Andrew looked

up and saw she was gazing out of the window. She couldn't see the farm from here. But he knew from the look on Gemma's face that she had it in mind – the locked gate and the endless wire, the rows of huge brown sheds.

Suddenly the blood rushed to her cheeks. She stabbed the brightly coloured book fiercely with her finger.

'If it's not *true*,' she cried, 'if it's not like this, why do people give us these books? Why do they try and trick us into thinking everything's fine and hunky-dory? This book is as bad as a lie! So why do they *do* it?'

Andrew prised her stiff, angry finger off the page of *On the Farm* before she made a hole. Then he turned the next page of the book the chicken gave him.

'Maybe,' he said, 'they don't want you to think about it.'

They read on.

4
I go chicken-dippy

I'd never been outside before. Never in my whole life. I went quite silly, really. I feel a bit of a fool even now, thinking back on it. But I went chicken-dippy. I couldn't handle it at all, not everything at once. Not when the only thing I'd known since I was hatched was wire netting and other chickens.

Try and imagine!

First, how it felt. All that wet air and wind. I'd never felt wind ruffling my feathers before. I'd never even been wet. Now here I was staggering about in a slimy mud puddle, stung by fierce little cold raindrops. It was so wonderful! It was like being born again. I felt I'd come *alive*!

And the noise! Roaring wind. Creaking tree tops. Deafening! The storm sounded like the world cracking in half, just for me, to wake me after a lifetime of having my ears stuffed with chicken cackle. I wanted to do my bit, so I joined in, clucking and squawking like something gone loopy.

Being outside in the fresh air was *great*.

And it was fresh. Fresh and cold. But what I'd never guessed was how many smells go to make up fresh air. Inside the shed was terrible – terrible! Too awful to describe. And at weekends, when we weren't cleaned out, it was even worse. The workers always wore masks, but even so, on some mornings they coughed and choked, and their eyes were red-rimmed.

(Imagine how *we* felt. We'd been in there all night!)

Outside, I smelled a thousand things I

couldn't even name until later – the leaf-mould underfoot, wet bracken, a thread of exhaust fumes from the road behind, cow parsnip, smoke from the chimney over the hill, the film of oil on the puddles.

A giant stew. Smells of the World! And I was breathing it for the first time. Me – a bedraggled, middle-aged feather baby.

But I felt *good*.

And there was so much to feel good about. Everywhere I looked were things I'd never seen. Inside the shed it's bright lights or total dark. Here, if I looked one way, I could see the eerie green glow of the spaceship. The other way, I saw the silver gleam of moonlight slicing through cloud, shadows and darker shadows. Ripples over the puddle. Dark grasses doubled in the wind, but still higher than my head. And, on the ground –

On the ground –

Peck! Peck! Peck! Peck!

Don't think I usually eat at night. (I
hope I know better than that!) But if you've

never ever had the chance to pick your food out of the ground – dig out a seed here, spot a bit of root there, pounce on a grub . . .

And, boy, did it taste good! If you, like me, had spent your life eating the same old dry pellets day after day, you'd understand how something fresh, something juicy, something wriggling and alive, could taste so perfect. Perfect!

Oh, try to imagine! I was wet. I was cold. And (now I look back on it) I think I must have been terrified.

But I was ecstatic! I was *free*!

And like all the other hens, I was hoping to stay so. By now, of course, everyone else had sensibly taken off. Some hid in the bushes the farmer had planted to try to hide the sheds from the road. The ones that hadn't rubbed too many feathers off on their cage wire managed to get up in the tree to roost. And I, too, staggered off in search of shelter.

(You'll not believe this.)

THE WRONG WAY!

Yes! Call me feather-brained! Call me chicken-dippy! Everyone else makes for the safety of black night. I go for the eerie green light! I make for the spaceship!

I have the thinking power of a vegetable, truly I do. I go and roost right under one of its gleaming sides.

And that is why I am the only one to hear, down the ventilation shaft, two of the little green men having a chat.

LGM 1: 'So what's for dinner?'

LGM 2: 'Not chicken, anyway!'

(They fell about laughing at this one, you could tell.)

LGM1: 'People?'

LGM2: 'You'll be lucky. We haven't even cleaned out the cages yet, let alone filled them up again.'

LGM1: 'So it's boring old breads, seeds, grains, beans, cheese, eggs, salads and vegetables and stuff, is it?'

LGM2: 'Don't knock 'em. Tasty and good for you.'

LGM1: 'But people taste so much better!'

LGM2: 'Oh, don't I know it! I agree. There's simply nothing to beat a nice roasting joint of –'

A metal door banged and I heard no more.

Oh, boy. Oh, boy oh boy!

Down on the muddy ground, under the ventilation shaft of the spaceship, I stood as if rooted, two totally different feelings fighting under my feathers.

(1) The sheer dancing joy of sweet revenge. See how you like it, people! Serves you right!

(2) Horror that others might suffer as I had.

Oh, which of these feelings would triumph? Which would win?

5

Penguins or cheetahs, whales or sharks

All morning Gemma had chicken on the brain. The moment the first lesson started, Andrew slid the little sacking book safely into his desk, and both of them were kept busy. But just from glancing at some of the mistakes in Andrew's workbook –

the cluck said 9.45

she put the coop on the saucer

Jane cycled feather than Jilly

– Gemma knew that he, too, wouldn't rest till he'd read on, and found out what had happened next on that black night at Harrowing Farm.

Would the chicken decide on revenge? Or on pity?

It wasn't easy to guess. What did

Gemma know about what a chicken thought or how a chicken felt? The closest she came to them was when she found one sitting quietly on her plate, crisply roasted or steaming in sauce.

She leaned across to nudge Andrew.

'Do you realise,' she told him, 'that there must be millions and millions of chickens all over the world, and I don't know anything about them.'

'You should watch the animal programmes on telly.'

'They never do chickens.'

Didn't they? Now Andrew came to think about it, Gemma was right. Almost every evening you could watch a programme about penguins or cheetahs, whales or sharks. You saw them hunting, sleeping, giving birth. But when did you ever get to see the day-to-day life of a chicken?

Never.

'You don't get stuffed chickens, either,' Gemma was telling him now.

'Yes, you do. I ate one yesterday.'

'No, no!' Gemma sounded quite angry with him. 'I mean soft furry toys. You're given teddy bears and pandas. You get tigers and cats and ponies. You might even get three fluffy yellow chicks in a nest especially at Easter. But no one ever gives you a hen.'

True. Under his bed at home Andrew still had Snoopy and Topcat and Dobbin and Grizzly. But for the life of him he couldn't remember ever ripping the bright shiny paper off a present, and shouting: 'Oh, goody! It's a hen!'

Gemma was getting angrier by the

minute.

'In fact,' she was muttering, 'when I come to think about it, I know more about *dinosaurs* than I do about hens. I know more about *hairy mammoths*. I know more about *pterodactyls*!'

Her usual little placid face had gone quite hard with rage. He knew her well enough to know what she was thinking. She couldn't bring the words out, so he said it for her.

'Because people don't have to be so ashamed about those. They're already dead.'

And suddenly neither of them could wait a moment longer to find out what happened next. Carefully, under cover of his workbook, Andrew slid the chicken's testament out of his desk.

They took it in turns to keep watch, as they read on.

6

I show myself to be naturally chicken-hearted

Revenge! Oh, ho, ho, ho. The very idea was ridiculous. Chickens aren't built for revenge. We don't have it in us. We're not the sort to slink about for years, feeling bitter, and then, when the moment comes, plunge in the sharpened claw.

We're a bit bird-witted, really. We mess about, scratching through each day as it comes. By daylight the only thing on my mind was breakfast, and I was out there peck-peck-pecking. I wouldn't even have noticed I was back near the sheds, except for the horrible wailing . . .

'Let me ooooouuuut!'

'Heeee-eeelp! Heeee-eeeelp!'

Oh, it was ghastly. Some creatures

make your flesh creep when they cry. Rabbits, for example. And baby hares.

But people!

'Saaaaave us, pleeeeaaase!'

Quick workers, these little green men. While I was roosting overnight, they must have pulled all the wire cages apart, and set them up again, exactly the right size.

(Of course, when I say, 'exactly the right size' . . .)

You couldn't help feeling sorry for them. There they sat, squashed in so tight they couldn't stand. They couldn't stretch. They couldn't turn around. Their pale faces pressed up against the cage bars.

'What's going to happen to us?'

'Let me out!'

'Oooooh!'

'Help us, *please*!'

Oh, it was pitiful. But they were one up on us poor chickens. They could at least argue with their jailors.

'Why are you keeping us in here? Are you planning to *eat* us?'

''Fraid so.'

'But that's *outrageous*.'

The little green man busy filling their water troughs was clearly a bit put out to hear this.

'What's so outrageous about it? You taste *good*.'

'You can't just eat us because we taste good!'

'Why not?'

'Because we're *people*, that's why.'

The little green man shrugged.

'Pigs. Chickens. People. What's the difference?'

'Pigs and chickens are only animals.'

'So? You're only people.'

'But we're *superior*.'

'Not to me, Buster,' said the little green man. And scowling horribly, he left the shed. When he came back, he brought a mate with him, to give him a hand with the water troughs.

'These people here,' he said, pointing to the inmates of the cages. 'They say they're superior.'

'Not to me, they're not,' his friend scoffed.

'That's what I told 'em!' laughed the first little green man.

The people were rattling their cage bars in a fury.

'We are! We are!'

'Superior? Come off it!' The little green man lifted his hand and ticked his points off, one by one, on some of his willowy green fingers.

'Horses are stronger. Swans are more loyal. Chimps live more peaceably. Seahorses have more babies. Dogs follow a scent better. Giraffes are taller. Squids have better eyesight. Camels go longer without water. Jaguars run faster. And little green men know more languages.'

He had plenty of fingers left, but he'd got bored.

'I could go on and on,' he said, picking up the last bucket and tipping the water smoothly into the last trough. 'In fact, I could be quite rude, and say that the only thing you lot really had going for you was that you ran the whole planet.'

Just before he slammed the shed door behind him, he added as an afterthought:

'Oh, yes! And you taste better than chicken!'

7

'Not today, thank you.'

'I won't have the chicken, thank you,' Gemma said to the dinner lady. 'Not today. Can I have what Vinit is having?'

The dinner lady made her usual joke.

'If Vinit doesn't eat up his meat, he won't grow.'

Vinit gave his usual polite chuckle. He was the tallest boy in the class, and had never eaten meat in his whole life. Today, Gemma and Andrew sat down on either side of him. Gemma seemed to have chicken on her mind, even if she had none on her plate.

'You've never eaten it *ever*?'

'No.'

'What about lamb?'

'No.'

'Pork?'

'No. We don't eat meat at all. No one in my family does. We never have.'

He watched as Gemma peeled open her sandwich hopefully, to see if the peanut butter was any thicker in the middle.

Across the table, Leila finished her mouthful and spoke up.

'My mum says that if we didn't eat animals, there would soon be hardly any of them about.'

Simon looked round in surprise when he heard this.

'My dad says if we didn't eat them, they'd overrun us in no time.'

'They can't both be right.'

'Maybe they're both wrong.'

The whole table fell quiet, thinking about people and animals. Whales. Dolphins. Elephants. Gorillas. Hard to believe that any animal in the world would be all that much worse off left alone.

Moodily, Andrew poked at the lump of chicken on his plate. He was hungry, but he couldn't quite bring himself to eat it. Gemma felt sorry for him. She didn't feel like swapping plates, but she did try to encourage him.

'I don't see why you shouldn't eat it if you want. That chicken was keen enough to gobble up the grub. And that was still alive.'

Vinit was staring now.

'What are you two on about? What chicken? What grub?'

'Nothing.'

'Doesn't matter.'

Andrew made another stab at eating his lunch. This time the fork got as far as his mouth before he had to put it down again.

Vinit was still staring at him.

'What's the matter?'

Andrew laid down his fork.

'I just can't eat it.'

'Why not?'

'I don't know. I think it's because I'm not sure where it comes from. I don't know how it fetched up on my plate. I don't know anything at all about it. I don't even know what sort of life it led.'

He looked gravely at Gemma.

'Maybe it even came out of one of those long brown sheds . . .'

Vinit was grinning now.

'If you can't eat it because you didn't know it personally,' he said, 'then you'd better have some of my sandwich.'

Gratefully, Andrew took what he was

offered. Silently, Gemma handed him some more. While he was chewing, he eyed the slab of chicken cooling on his plate.

'I'd eat it,' he told Gemma and Vinit, 'I'd eat it with no trouble if I knew for certain that all its life it had been –'

He broke off. It sounded so silly that he couldn't say it.

'Yes?' Vinit prompted him. 'You'd eat it if you knew that all its life it had been –?'

Andrew blushed.

'Happy as a grub.'

'A *grub*? You mean, like a *maggot*?'

Andrew nodded.

Vinit laid down what was left of his sandwich, and pushed back his chair.

'Excuse me,' he said politely, and got up and left.

Without even thinking, Andrew snatched up the remains of Vinit's sandwich, and gobbled it.

'Hungry work, all this reading,' he explained to Gemma.

8
Chicken no longer!

I stuck my beady eye to a knothole. Inside the shed, an argument was raging.

'Listen, you don't *need* to eat us. You got on perfectly well before you landed here. None of you look starved. None of you even look hungry. Why pick on us?'

'I *told* you. You *taste* good. After a long, hard day taking over a new planet, there's absolutely nothing to beat the smell of a nice, roasting –'

'Shut up! Shut up!'

All the cage bars were rattled frantically.

'Stop saying that!'

'Not in front of the children!'

The little green man

43

tried to be reasonable.

'Look,' he said. 'I grant you it isn't the world's best life, being stuck in a cage till you're eaten. And maybe we were a bit rough with one or two of you. I'm sorry about that.' He spread his green hands. 'There. I've said it. I'm sorry. I can't say fairer than that, can I?'

He waited for his apology to be accepted as generously and graciously as he had made it.

There was a stony silence. Then, from the back row of cages came the word:

'X!*&@/%!'

Language a chicken wouldn't dream of repeating.

The little green man's mood turned a shade on the ugly side.

'I'll tell you what gets me,' he said. 'The sheer hypocrisy of it! Who built these sheds without any windows or fresh air? You

lot did! Who put up the cages? You did! And who locked those poor stupid little chickens up in them?'

('Poor stupid little chickens'? I didn't care much for his attitude. But I kept watching.)

He was swinging around now, pointing a green finger at cage after cage.

'And who kept them in here, not just day after day, or week after week, but for *lifetimes*?' His green lip curled with scorn. 'Now look at you! The tables are turned, and do any of you have the guts to face the fact you're getting no worse than you gave out? No. It's moan, moan, moan! Weep, weep, weep! Whine, whine, whine! You *disgust* me!'

He glowered round the shed.

'Want to know something?' he said. (They clearly didn't, but he told them anyway.) 'Your sort really make me sick! Even the chickens took it better than you do!'

(I still didn't care for his tone, if I'm truthful.)

Someone behind him started arguing again.

'But it wasn't so bad for the chickens. They're not as *sensitive* as we are.'

The little green man's eyes widened.

'That's a good one,' he said, almost admiringly. 'Is that how you did it? Is that what you kept telling yourselves?' He grinned from green ear to green ear. '*We* could try that one,' he said. 'We're sending the spaceship back tonight, to fetch a few spices and a much bigger casserole dish. If anyone up there starts feeling sorry for you lot, I'll try that one on them.'

Tipping his head to one side, he waved his willowy green fingers and said in a very silly fashion:

'Oh, don't you worry about those *people*. They're all right. I know they squawk and fuss and rattle the cage bars, trying to get out. But, honestly, they don't mind really. You see, they're not nearly as *sensitive* as we are!'

And then he fell about laughing.

Another time, I might have had a little private cackle at this joke. But not right that minute. You see, just then I'd come to a decision. Quite a brave decision for a chicken. I think I've mentioned that we lot aren't really built for revenge. Well, if I'm honest, we're not a byword for courage, either. We're not daredevils. We're not desperadoes. The name 'chicken' in fact (you may not know this) has almost come to mean 'faint heart' or 'a bit of a funker'.

No need to mince words. We chickens tend to have cold feet.

But call me chicken no longer! For I had decided on a plan so bold, so daring, so foolhardy, I frankly doubted if anyone, anywhere, would ever truly think of me as chicken again.

I'd stow away on the spaceship.

Yes! Yes! I'd fly a frillion miles, to outer space! Tell everyone on the planets exactly what was going on!

Surely, oh, *surely*, as soon as all the little green families out there heard about the horrible cages and learned what was happening, to feed *them*, they'd stick to eating boring old breads, seeds, grains, beans, cheese, eggs, salads and vegetables.

And maybe the odd happy grub or two . . .

9
Just a toy

'So *brave* . . .'

Gemma was bursting with admiration as she waited for Andrew to reach the bottom of the page.

He lifted his head, distracted.

'Brave? Who?'

'The chicken, of course! Who else?'

Andrew took a moment to answer. Then he said:

'I don't know. It all seems very odd. I'm not sure if I believe it. I mean, here's this farm, almost next door to the school. We've lived here all our lives, and never heard anyone say a word about the place. Not once.'

'So?'

'So how can it be that bad? If it was

that bad, surely people would be *talking* about it.'

What he said bothered Gemma. Was he right? She stabbed her finger on the chicken's book, to get him reading again, so they could both turn over. But while he laboriously worked his way down the page of scratchy writing, she thought about what he'd said. And as soon as he reached the last line and looked up, she was sitting there ready to argue.

'I'll tell you how. Because they don't notice what they do, just so long as they're the ones doing it!'

'Who? Chickens?'

'No. Adults, of course! Think about it. If we did some of the things they do, they would be horrified. Suppose some of us took horses and rode them so fast in a race over such high and dangerous fences that, every year, some of them crashed down on the other side and broke their legs and had to be shot. They would go mad at us! They'd say our parents weren't looking after us properly. They'd take us into care.'

She was right.

'They would, too.'

'And suppose you were poking about at an animal as if it were just a toy, and you wanted to look at the clockwork inside it. You'd get in such trouble! You couldn't just put a white coat on, and say, "I only wanted to know what would happen if I did this, or that". "*I'm curious*" isn't any better excuse for poking at things than "*I'm spiteful*"!'

'No,' Andrew agreed with her. 'Not if you're the one getting poked.'

Gemma took a deep breath.

'I'll tell you something,' she said. 'I don't think this chicken is just *brave*. I think this chicken is a *saint*.'

He tried to hide his smile, but it was too late. She had seen it.

'No, really!' she insisted. 'If I'd been treated this way by people, I'd be *glad* to see them stuffed in my old cage. I would! I wouldn't risk what was left of my life flying frillions of miles to try and save them.'

Her look was fierce.

'I would let them *roast*!'

And before he could even begin to argue, she'd flipped the page over and carried on reading.

10

Green sky. Green earth. Green wind. Green sand.

Take my advice. Don't ever stow away in a spaceship. You'll have the worst time ever.

They go faster than light. The soothing hum of the engines keeps lulling you off into daydreams. And when you try and distract yourself by peering out of the porthole, all you can see is crazy glittering spirals of shooting stars, blazing fireballs, bright spinning planets and shimmering flares of comet tails.

I nearly *died* of boredom. Honestly. By the time we came down (or up, or in, or over – hard to tell which), I was almost ready to give myself up, and hope they were all still sick of eating chicken.

But the planet itself was wonderful. It was green. Green sky. Green earth. Green wind. Green sand. (We landed on the beach.) Not being green, I scuttled off as fast as I could, into the undergrowth. That was green too. So were the seeds and roots. So were the grubs. And just in case you never get the chance to eat a green grub, I'll tell you now, they are the *best*. Mmmmm-*mmmmm*! Skin just a little bit crunchy, like a thin crust. And inside – so creamy and rich! Beak-smacking good!

And they're not very bright. I caught forty.

Then it was time to get on with the job.

I set off down the green road. I'd only

walked round a couple of bends before I came across a huge advertisement set up to catch the eye of anyone walking the same way as I was.

I stared in horror. I'd picked up enough of the language on the trip to know exactly what it said:

HUNGRY?
Just one more mile to

PEOPLE IN A BASKET

Baked, roast, broiled, stuffed, stewed, breaded in bite-sized chunks.
We do 'em any way you like 'em!

Opening Friday with a Special Offer
Free green chips and green salad!

Above the sign was a picture of a farm, filled with happy people of all ages and sizes running around a sunny meadow, laughing and eating ice creams. Under the picture was the slogan:

ALL OUR PEOPLE ARE
FARM-FRESH

I stood rooted to the spot. I was horrified. Farm-fresh, indeed! I'm not *daft*. I knew that anyone who arrived in time to be cooked for the grand opening on Friday had to come out of those horrid cramped cages.

Sunny meadows! Ice cream!

'Ha!'

'I beg your pardon?'

I must have cackled it aloud, because the little green man who was hurrying up behind me now said again:

'I beg your pardon?'

It seemed as good a time as any to start on my mission of mercy.

'This sign!' I said. 'This advert for

ALL OUR PEOPLE ARE
FARM-FRESH

"People In A Basket". It's all *lies*. Terrible lies! These people don't frolic about in sunny meadows. They don't run around smiling and eating ice creams. It's not like that at all. I know the truth. I've been there, and seen it, and it isn't like that. These people are locked up in dark little cages. They don't get any fresh air. There's no daylight. These people –'

I broke off. The little green man was flapping his hands at me so frantically his fingers were rippling.

'Don't tell me!' he said. 'I don't want to hear about it. I don't want to know.'

He was laughing.

'You'll spoil my dinner!'

11
'No fear!'

'I wouldn't mind being eaten.'

Gemma stared.

Andrew was gazing thoughtfully out of the window. Then he turned and said it again.

'I've been thinking about it, and I honestly don't think I'd mind being eaten.'

She thought about it too. Maybe to help her along, and maybe just to amuse himself, he kept suggesting recipes.

'Fried Gemma,' he said. 'Gemma on toast. Curried Gemma. Sweet and sour Gemma slices. Gemma and chutney sandwich. Spaghetti Gemma.'

Now she was laughing, so he asked:

'What do you think?'

She shook her head.

'No fear!'

'But why not?'

'I'll show you why not.' Opening her desk, she pulled out one of her old workbooks. Andrew watched as she flicked steadily back through the pages till she reached a block graph they'd done the term before.

She spread the pages open.

'See?'

He took a look.

'So what's the problem?' he asked her.

'What's the problem?' She shook her head at him as if he were an idiot. 'The problem is obvious. I'm thinking I might end up in the pot a bit *early*.'

But Andrew couldn't see it.

'Look,' he argued. 'This graph says *seven* for a chicken, right? We had chicken last Sunday. I was with Dad when he bought it. He was looking for one that weighed exactly four pounds. The shop boy saw Dad peering at the labels, and told him, "They're all nice and young and tender, about seven weeks old", and . . .'

Andrew's voice trailed away.

Gemma had lifted her finger from the workbook. Now he could see the last two words of the title.

The Natural Life Span of Animals in Years.

'Oh,' he said. '*Years.*' He had another think. Then he said to Gemma:

'All right. I've changed my mind. I wouldn't mind being eaten, but only if it was a bit fairer.'

'Fairer?'

'You know,' he said. 'Not just arranged so I was born, kept tidily out of sight till I had grown to a useful size that fits exactly on everybody's fridge shelf, then shoved neatly in a wrapper as if I wasn't really a living animal at all. As if it was just some sort of *factory*, and I was just –'

He paused.

'As if you were just what?' Gemma asked him.

'A *thing*. As if I were just a *thing.*'

'You're right,' said Gemma. 'I wouldn't mind then, either. If I'd had a reasonably good time, and it had lasted a fair while, I wouldn't mind being eaten.'

They sat quietly for a while, thinking of interesting recipes for one another.

Then they went back to their reading.

12
Chicken of history

Fortune favours the feathery. What luck it was that the little green man hurrying along the road at my side turned out to be big in television.

I flapped along, trying to keep up. (I won't go on about my feet, but after my time in those cages I'm a *martyr* to footcurl.)

'Half an hour,' he kept moaning. 'Only half an hour! That's all the time I have left.'

I couldn't think what he meant. Was he ill? Surely not. He looked perfectly fit and green.

'All the time left for what?' I asked.

'To find a celebrity guest for tonight.' He glanced down at me. 'Have you dropped out of the *sky*?' he asked. 'You can't have been here long, or you'd recognise me. I'm the host of a famous television chat show.' He started to walk even faster. 'A chat show without a celebrity guest! I had a singer this morning. But she fell sick. I know she's not shamming because she keeps turning pink. Then I found this fellow who doesn't glow in the dark.'

He broke off and looked down at me again.

'Can you *believe* it? It sounds incredible, doesn't it? But it's true. This fellow doesn't glow in the dark. Not one bit!'

'Hard to believe,' I cackled politely, though I was out of breath from keeping up with him.

'Isn't it? But he says he won't come on the show. Personally, I think he's chicken.'

I was a bit put out by this insensitivity.

'Shame . . .' I said frostily.

The little green man caught my tone.

He glanced down. Then he looked again. Then he gave me a steady green-eyed stare.

The idea in his mind slowly dawned in mine.

Go on, I willed him silently. *Go on! Invite me!* (My big chance!)

'You wouldn't . . .' he began tentatively, rippling his fingers in his embarrassment. 'You wouldn't be here doing something interesting, would you, by any chance? Something that might appeal to my viewers?'

I almost *crowed*.

'*Everyone* watches,' he assured me anxiously. 'Everyone on the whole planet. I tell you, at seven tonight there'll be frillions of them sitting on their sofas, all waiting to see who will be guest celebrity on my chat show.'

He leaned down, his eyes deep green pools of hope.

'No chance you might . . . you could . . .?'

He shook his little green head, and hurried on.

'No,' he said. 'Silly of me to ask . . .'

I puffed out my chest. We Chickens of History must seize our moments where we may.

'Little Green Man,' I declared. 'You are in luck. I am the ideal guest for your chat show. Not only –' (and here I couldn't help ruffling up my feathers a little from sheer pride) – 'not only do I not glow in the dark – no, not one bit! – but I am here on a Mission.'

'A Mission? Really?'

'A Mission of Mercy.'

'Fancy that!'

'I have a Message, in fact.'

His eyes gleamed. I could tell just from looking at the expression on his face that he thought that sounded good. I knew what was running through his little green mind. 'Tonight, Viewers, I have as my celebrity guest someone very, very special: A Chicken on a Mission of Mercy. A Chicken with a Message.'

'A Message for everyone on this planet,' I told him.

His eyes gleamed greener.

'Now that is really something,' he breathed. 'You don't glow in the dark, and you have a Message for everyone on the planet.'

'And the Message is –'

He clamped his long green fingers round my beak.

'No!' he cried. 'Don't say it! Save it for the show, or you'll go stale!'

Go stale! Really! I flapped after him, shaking my head in amazement. They

might be superior, these little green men; but they obviously didn't know it all.

Go stale, indeed! What did he think I was? A loaf of *bread*?

13

Been done before

It was Andrew who was caught poring over the book and told to put whatever he was reading back in his desk while he got on with his work.

For a while he slaved away at his project on water plants. But the chicken was on his mind, and in the end he whispered to Gemma:

'What do you think the Message to the planet is?'

Gemma's eyes flashed. She was

certainly ready with an answer. He realised suddenly that this was what she'd been thinking about while she waited for him to reach the bottom of the page.

'I hope,' she said fiercely, 'I hope the chicken tells them that those poor things in the cages are living creatures, just like they are, and ought to be treated exactly the same!'

'Not exactly the same, Gemma.'

She turned her fierce look on him.

'Why not?'

He shrugged.

'It might be silly. After all, we don't know anything about the little green people, do we? Maybe they stay awake and do arithmetic all night, so they'll feel nice and fresh in the morning. Maybe they like having their birthday parties in mud puddles. Maybe they enjoy having their faces slapped. It's a bit risky to tell them to treat everyone exactly the same. I'd wait till I knew more about them.'

But Gemma wasn't put off.

'There's no problem,' she told Andrew sternly. 'They can treat them exactly the same. They can treat them *well*. They treat themselves well, don't they?'

'But we don't know what that *means*!'

She was really impatient with him now, you could tell.

'Oh, Andrew! Don't you see? It doesn't really matter what it means. Everyone's different. If you're a child, it probably means keeping you safe and happy, and making sure you go to school. If you're one of the little green people it probably means letting you sit on the sofa and watch your favourite chat show. And if you're a chicken, it means letting you outside in the fresh air to peck your own food, and giving you somewhere a bit private and comfy to lay your eggs. That's all.'

Fair enough, thought Andrew. Sounds quite reasonable. Shouldn't be too difficult. Been done before. (That was quite obvious from *On the Farm*.)

And since they weren't being watched any longer, he slid the book the chicken gave him out of the desk, and together they carried on reading.

14
Chat show chicken

The lights! The cameras! The fanfare! The curving steps! (I had a little trouble with the steps.) Then the wing-shake! And the green velvet sofa!

'Tonight, Viewers,' said my little green host proudly. 'Tonight – a great treat! A Chicken with a Mission. Not only does she not glow in the dark – Don't go away! We'll be seeing that later! – but she is here with a Message.'

He turned to me.

'Tell us the Message, Chicken.'

I turned to the cameras. I told them all the story of my life. I told them about the dreadful sheds, and who was in them now. I pointed out that it didn't even make *sense*.

'Why not?' my host demanded. 'After all, everyone has to eat.'

'Yes,' I said. 'But, you see, you're not just stuffed in the cages. While you're in the cages, you're stuffed! Stuffed with food.'

'What's wrong with that?' he demanded.

'What's wrong with that,' I told him and frillions of others, 'is that if you're going to be eaten (and it doesn't matter what you are – pig, chicken, calf, it's all the same) you have to grow. And to grow, you have to eat. In fact, you have to eat loads and loads to grow big enough for anyone to want to bother to eat *you*. So whoever ends up with you on their plate could just have eaten *your* food in the first place.'

'And what's your food?'

'Cereal stuffs and vegetables.'

He made a face.

'Boring old cereal stuffs and vegetables!'

I ignored him.

'And then they could have invited a whole crowd of other hungry people to join

them. Because if you're going to be eaten you have to eat practically *ten whole fields* full of corn and stuff to make as much good food out of yourself as there was in just *one* of those fields to begin with.'

'Really?' my little green host said, stifling a yawn. 'I wonder how many of my viewers knew that.'

He turned to the camera.

'Hello, out there!' he said. 'Calling all hungry viewers! It looks as if the chicken's Message is as follows. Gang up with nine others. Pounce on one meat-eater. Force the meat-eater to eat fields instead. And all your problems will be over.'

And he fell off his green sofa, laughing.

I never thought my Mission would be easy. Indifference. Danger. Ridicule. Chickens of History must face them all. I could have sulked. I could have pushed the microphone aside with my wing and strutted off the set in disgust. I could have wept.

But no.

I kept my head and my dignity.

'I see I'm not getting my Message over too well,' I told my little green host. 'So allow me to offer your viewers something more on their wavelength. I'll show them how I don't glow in the dark.'

The green glint in his eyes said:

'Now that's a bit more like it, Chicken. That might just save this wash-out show.'

His soft honey voice said:

'That would be *wonderful*, wouldn't it, Viewers?'

I fluttered down from the sofa and spread my wings.

The studio lights dimmed.

'Now I need total darkness, please.'

Suddenly there was total darkness.

In it, I silently, sadly, crept away.

15
In front of frillions

'Poor, poor chicken.'

'How awful!'

'Oh, how she must have felt.'

'On television, too.'

'In front of frillions.'

'Well, at least she tried.'

'Poor, poor chicken.'

16
Chicken Celebrity

I woke up famous.

I didn't know it, of course. (I'd roosted quietly somewhere behind Broadcasting Orb.) But it seems all night the phones had been ringing. ('Play it again!' 'Action replay!') No one could work out how the trick had been done. No one could believe their eyes. A chicken who really didn't glow in the dark? Not one bit? ('Oh, please show that one more time.' 'Action replay!')

I lost count of my media appearances. I was on *The Late Show*. I was on *The News*. And *Your Planet Tonight*. And *Good Morning, Green People*! Since I was invited on to everything, I soon made it a rule that I had to be given five minutes for my Mission of Mercy, my Message to the planet, before I wouldn't glow in the dark.

And I quickly learned what makes good television. After all, the last thing I wanted was for all the little green frillions to rush off to make tea, or visit the lavatory, while I was doing my chat bit.

So I invented lots of little rhymes, to keep the viewers' attention.

'If you don't know how to treat 'em,
Then you shouldn't really eat 'em,'

I might tell my delighted audience. Or:

'If they're cramped in a cage,
It should put you in a rage.'

You could always tell when the interviewer had a secret soft spot for a nice Sunday roast.

'Surely they must be happy in the cages, or they wouldn't put on weight,' she would try to argue.

'Nonsense!' I'd say, flapping my wings. 'Look at me! I was *miserable*. And I got bigger. I even laid eggs! If you have nothing to do all day but eat, then you eat. And if you're forced to sit on your bum because no one wants you running around getting thinner, then you get nice and plump. Doesn't mean that you're *happy*.'

I'd wink at the camera.

'If you can't see them playing,
Then you shouldn't be paying!'
I chanted.

'It doesn't *hurt* them, though, does it?' she'd insist.

'Cutting all your beautiful green hair off wouldn't hurt you,' I'd point out. 'It would still make you very unhappy, if you wanted to keep it.'

Another wink at the camera, in case the audience was flagging.

'My chat show hostess needs her hair.

Chickens and people need fresh air!'

You could tell that my little green interviewer was getting impatient with me now. She wanted to get on to the not-glowing-in-the-dark bit.

'Can't be too bad, can it?' she'd say tartly. 'Or it would have been stopped already.'

I'd wrap my wings round my chest, and lean urgently towards the camera.

'That's a very interesting point,' I'd say. 'Try and look at it this way. Suppose one of you frillions of viewers out there kept one of these poor pink people as a pet at home. Suppose you stuffed them in a tiny cage and never let them out. What would happen?'

I'd pause while they thought about it.

'That's right!' I'd say, after a moment. 'Everyone would say it was cruel. Your neighbours would be disgusted. Your family would quarrel with you. And if *you* did nothing about it, then *they* would. They'd unlock the cage door, or phone the RSPCPP.'

I'd flap my wings in my excitement.

'But if lots of people do it, just to make sure you get bigger and cheaper helpings on your plate of something you don't even need to eat, *then* what happens?'

I'd turn to the little green interviewer.

'Frillions as sensitive and intelligent as you just go along with it. Stick up for the whole idea, even! It's just amazing! And it's time things changed.'

She'd shift in her chair. She was getting quite irritable now.

'Talking of time,' she'd say. 'The minutes are ticking by. After the break,

we're going to meet the entire crew of the next space flight down to Chicken's home planet. But, right now, watch carefully, Viewers. Some of you may have seen this before, and not been able to believe your eyes. This chicken doesn't glow in the dark!'

Cue for the lights to dim, the drums to roll.

I'd slip off the sofa and spread my wings.

The cameras would focus carefully.

The lights would snap off.

And, for me, yet another show would be over.

17
Out it came

Gemma was looking at Andrew. Well, looking wasn't exactly the right word. She was staring in his direction, but she was obviously miles away.

Finally, out it came.

'Don't eat so many, don't eat so much,
Then they won't be kept as cramped as ten
*   rabbits in a hutch.'*

It didn't take him long to come back at her.

'Unlock the cage and open up the door,
If you really want to eat it, you must pay a
*   little more.'*

With honours now even, they could get back to their reading.

18
Surprises, surprises!

Behind me, as I crept away, I heard the crew of the spaceship chatting.

'Doesn't glow in the dark!'

'Must be some sort of trick.'

'Can't see it any more, anyway.'

'Where did it go?'

Where indeed? Where would you go if you'd done your very best – pleaded and persuaded, argued and explained – and you'd got nowhere?

You'd go home.

And that was my plan. I might have failed in my Mission of Mercy. I might not have managed to get my Message across to everyone on the planet, but I still had one thing going for me.

I didn't glow in the dark.

The spaceship was waiting, empty. Hadn't my little green interviewer boasted that she was talking to the entire crew? I would creep over, climb in and stow away for the long journey home.

Home! Oh, how I longed to be back again! It would be good to change green skies for blue, and not be pointed out in the street, or hear whispering everywhere I went. ('I've watched it *five times* now, and, do you know, I still can't work out how it's done!' 'You can see the whole thing again tonight, you know. At six o'clock. On *Planet People*.')

To be a private chicken again! Oh, I confess I was feeling quite weepy with relief as I dragged a few green weeds and stuff with me into the spaceship, and made a bit of a nest in the dark at the back of the radio cupboard.

Daft place to pick! The little green

space crew switched on the radio the moment they came in, and kept it on day and night.

I nearly went *mad*. I was about to burst out of the cupboard, clucking hysterically, when suddenly I heard something that rooted me even further down in my makeshift nest.

'And now!' the radio voice said. 'The results of our phone-in! This week the subject was: How We Treat People Before We Get Round To Roasting Them! The phone lines have been busy, busy, busy! And this is what you think!'

Was I *dreaming*?

No, I wasn't.

The radio voice took up the story.

'Surprises, surprises! Almost all of you think we ought to treat them better. Most of you said you were very shocked indeed by some of the things the chicken told you.

Over half of you would be prepared to pay a little more for your people-burgers if you thought they'd be happier before they fetched up on your little green plates. And quite a few of you said you were definitely going to try and eat less people and more breads and seeds and grains and bleh, bleh, bleh!'

He let out a huge, dramatic groan that echoed through the cupboard.

'Boring!'

Then he cheered up again.

'But the most astonishing surprise of all – chew on this, folks! A full ten per cent of you (yes, that's one in ten!) now truly believe that it wasn't a trick, and the chicken didn't glow in the dark.'

He whistled down the radio, almost deafening me.

'Can you *believe* that? What sort of nuts do we have listening to *Planet Phone-In*? Are one in ten of you *crazy*? Have a good look at the people beside you as we listen to the next record, 'Rooster Rag' by Billy Bantam and the Rednecks. And, after that, folks, we'll have the results of the poetry competition!'

I can't say, in all honesty, that on any other occasion I would have enjoyed listening to 'Rooster Rag'. But at that moment the efforts of Billy Bantam and the Rednecks sounded almost like music to my ears. What had the radio voice said? *Almost all* thought they ought to treat them better before they roasted them. *Most* were shocked by what they'd heard. *Over half* would pay more. *Quite a few* were going to try and eat more other things instead.

My Message to the planet had got through! I was overjoyed!

And in my ecstasy, I laid an egg.

Surprise, surprise!

Fool that I was to crow about it. The little green crew heard, and poked their heads into the cupboard.

'It's that chicken!'

'You!'

The captain shook his head in amazement.

'It's dark enough in there,' he said. 'And it definitely isn't glowing.'

'Not one bit.'

'Can't be a trick, then.'

'Weird!'

The row of little green heads peered at me curiously. Then one of them said:

'Call me a madman if you will, but if it doesn't glow in the dark, I'm not eating it.'

'Me neither.'

'Nor me.'

'I'm not if you three aren't.'

'That's it, then. No point in wringing its neck if we're not going to eat it.'

'None at all.'

'Just make the spaceship go whiffy.'

I was pretty relieved, I can tell you.

'Fancy a fresh egg?' I offered in a rush of generosity.

'No, thanks.'

'Not just at this moment.'

'Not if it's one of yours.'

I think there might have been a moment or two of slight unpleasantness, if 'Rooster Rag' hadn't suddenly drawn to a close, and the radio voice started up again.

'Competition Time! And the subject for your poems this week, as you all know, was "Roast People". So let's look at our three winners. Interestingly, none of you wrote about the glorious aroma seeping from the oven, or the crisp taste of the first mouthful. Let's see what you did write!'

A fanfare of trumpets sounded.

'Third prize! To George Green, of 27

Greenhill Lane, for:

Kind people always boast
That they chose a happy roast.

That's very good, George!'

There was another fanfare.

'Who's next? In second place we have
Gloria Greengage of Lower Greenfield, with:

Cruel farmers now must fear we all
Will switch to veg. and cereal.

Wonderful, Gloria! You've certainly earned
your dinner tonight!'

The third fanfare was the longest of all.

'And now! Our winner! Maria Greenacre of 41 The Green, and her winning poem:

If it doesn't smile a lot
Then it won't go in my pot.

Marvellous, Maria! Absolutely first-rate!'

Well may Maria Greenacre have felt
proud. But I felt prouder. Three winning
poems on the subject of 'Roast People',
and each of them could have been written

by myself: they were caring; they were sensitive; they were *humane*.

Three splendid poems.

All the way home I passed the time quoting them quietly in the cupboard. (I thought it wiser to stay out of sight.) Even when we landed, and the crew booted me unceremoniously off the spaceship –

'Go home, Chicken!'

'– absolutely sick of hearing it clucking away in that cupboard!'

'– have to air the whole spaceship!'

'– think itself lucky we didn't eat it . . .'

– I was still repeating the winning poem.

'If it doesn't smile a lot

Then it won't go in my pot.'

My Mission of Mercy was over. I was content.

19
The last few words

And there the book ended. The last few words strayed in their scratchy fashion across the page. The full stop was a tiny seed, pressed into the sacking. Underneath was a firm chicken's footprint.

The bell rang for the end of school.

20
Close them all

He knew that she would have to chum him home. She couldn't just stroll off her own way, not today, not after reading all that.

Together they went down the path beside the old farm. The sheds were obviously empty. The doors were banging in the wind.

There was no sign of the chicken. Every few yards they stopped to press their faces against the fence, and stare across.

Nothing.

Picking her way back to the path through the nettles, Gemma's foot struck something hard. She reached down, and with Andrew's help, prised a heavy old board out of the undergrowth.

HARROWING FARM

'There are others,' she told him. 'All over

the place there must still be other Harrowing Farms.'

'Not for much longer,' said Andrew. 'Not if everyone we know can help it.' He pointed through the fence. 'If a chicken can close one, the rest of us can close them all.'

'Open them, you mean.'

'Yes. Open them up.'

He caught her hands in his, and spun her round, yelling:

'*Let your chickens run around!*'

Quick as a flash, she yelled back:

'*Eggs are tastier if they can't be found!*'

They went off singing at the tops of their voices.

Behind, in the long grass, the chicken clucked with pride.